The Singing Snake

*For Anne and Tony Suche, who made me aware of Australian aboriginal
paintings and the many legends connected with them.*

Printed in China.
For more information address Hyperion Books for Children,
114 Fifth Avenue, New York, New York 10011.
First Hyperion Paperback edition: April 1995
1 3 5 7 9 10 8 6 4 2
Library of Congress Catalog Card Number: 92-85515
ISBN: 1-56282-399-X (trade)/1-56282-400-7 (lib. bdg.)/0-7868-1036-X (pbk.)

This book is set in 16-point Palatino.
The illustrations are prepared in gouache art medium.
Designed by A. O. Osen

The Singing Snake

STORY BY

STEFAN CZERNECKI AND **TIMOTHY RHODES**

ILLUSTRATED BY

STEFAN CZERNECKI

Hyperion Paperbacks for Children

New York

Long ago, on a great island in the middle of the ocean, there lived a collection of creatures found nowhere else in the world. They all chattered at once, and their voices were harsh and loud. The island was the noisiest place you could imagine.

Tired of the raucous sounds, Old Man said he would make a musical instrument in honor of the creature who developed the most beautiful singing voice. All day and all night the animals and birds sang and sang, each trying to sing louder than the others in order to be noticed by Old Man. The voices were more musical, but the sound of so many different animals singing at the same time made such a din that no one could sleep.

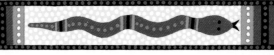

"Enough," said Old Man one day. "We will all gather together, have a proper contest, and settle this once and for all. I need some sleep."

A large, colorful snake listened to Old Man and thought about his chances. He wanted to win the contest, but he knew that he had only an average singing voice. It would never be judged the best. He listened carefully to the other contestants.

"Lark has the most beautiful voice," Snake finally decided.

Day after day Snake hid in the grass beneath the trees and listened to Lark sing. At night he went off by himself to practice. But no matter how hard he tried to imitate Lark's voice, the only result was a sore throat. After a while Snake knew that he would never win the contest. He became very jealous of Lark's voice.

One day Lark flew down from a tree near Snake and began to hop about on the ground, pecking at insects. Snake noticed how very small Lark was.

"Hmmm." He was getting an idea. "If I swallowed Lark whole and was careful not to harm her, and held her just at the back of my throat, then I'm sure I could *borrow* her voice for the song festival."

Once Snake had made up his mind, he quickly swallowed Lark. She began to sing in protest, but her song appeared to be coming from Snake.

This will work perfectly, thought Snake. He hastened off to the festival.

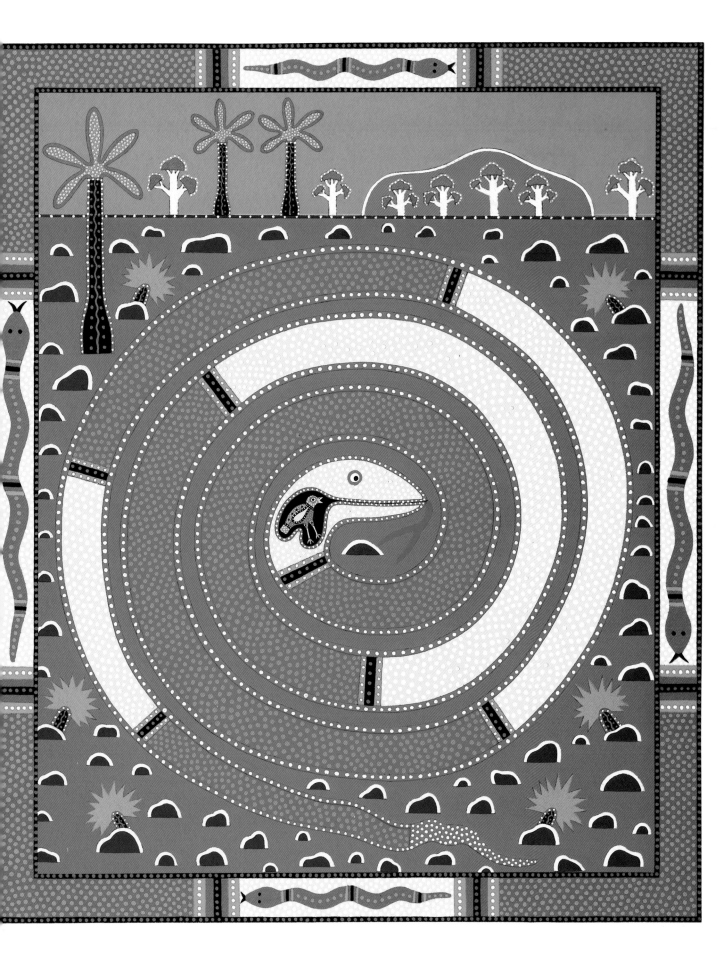

Whenever he encountered another animal along the way, Snake would smile, taking care that his teeth blocked Lark's escape.

When Snake smiled, the light shone through his teeth, and Lark began to sing.

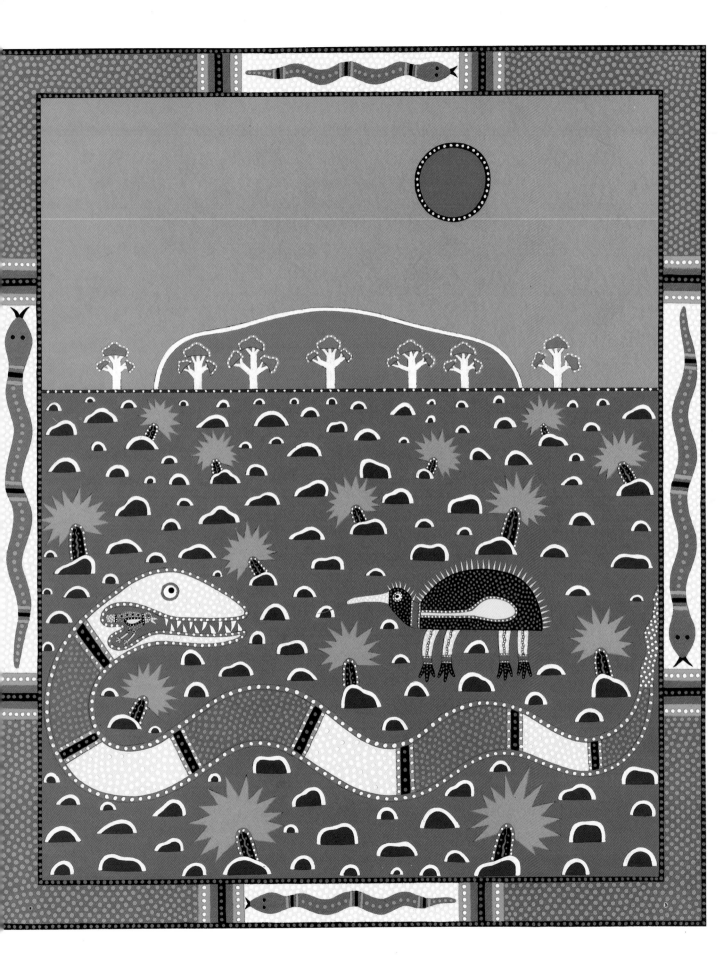

Everyone thought that Snake was singing, and they marveled at his magnificent voice.

"Your voice is certainly much improved from last year," said Platypus.

"Snake has obviously been taking singing lessons," remarked Lyrebird, somewhat peevishly.

"I wish I had a voice as enchanting as Snake's," whined Dingo.

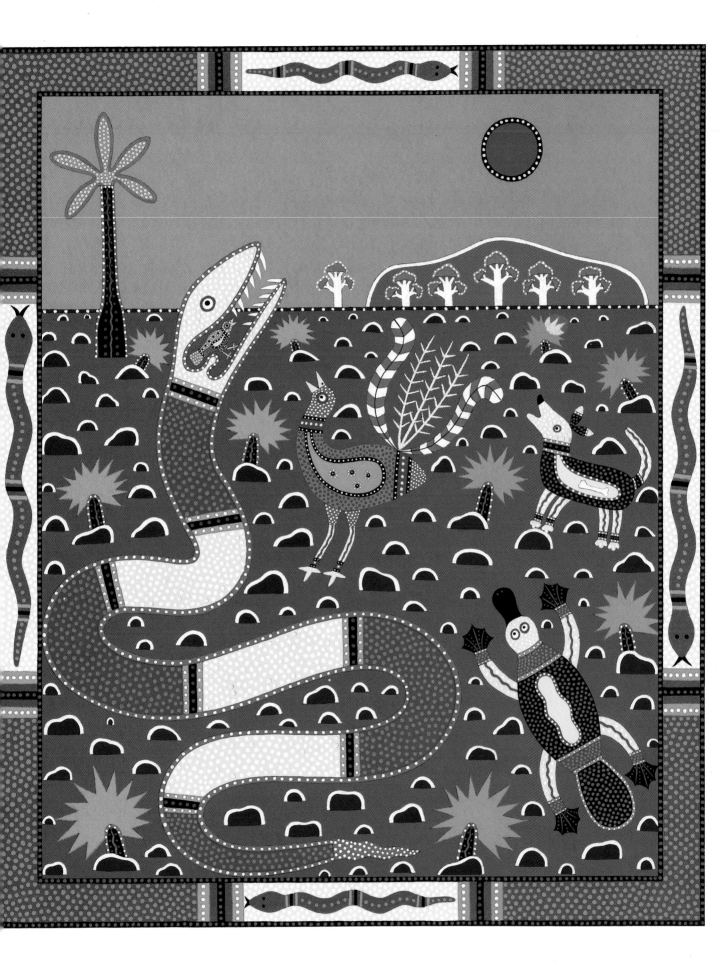

Snake smiled serenely and continued on his way. As he approached the festival, he met more and more creatures. They all expressed amazement at his brilliant voice. Even the other birds were filled with wonder when Snake sang.

"It's almost as if Snake were a bird," said Emu admiringly.

"Such a sorrowful and anguished song," added Cockatoo. "It makes me want to cry."

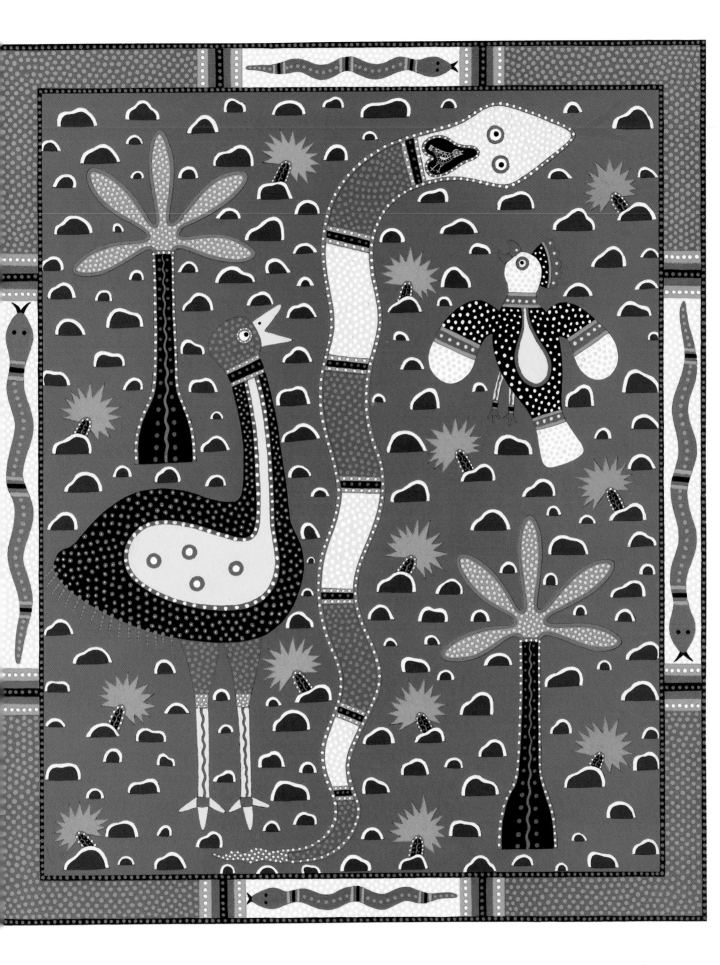

The song festival was ready to begin. When all the participants were assigned places on the program for the contest, Snake didn't wait his turn. He squeezed his way between Blue-tongued Lizard and Long-necked Tortoise to the front of the line. Then he reared himself up, held his head in the air, and smiled. The sunlight struck Lark, and she began to sing.

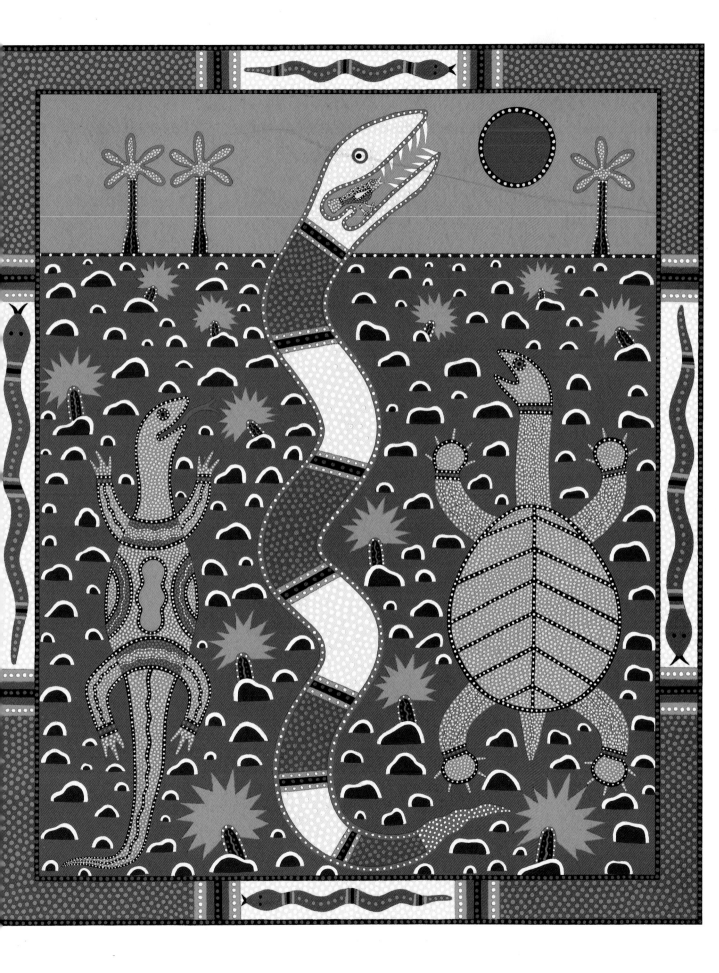

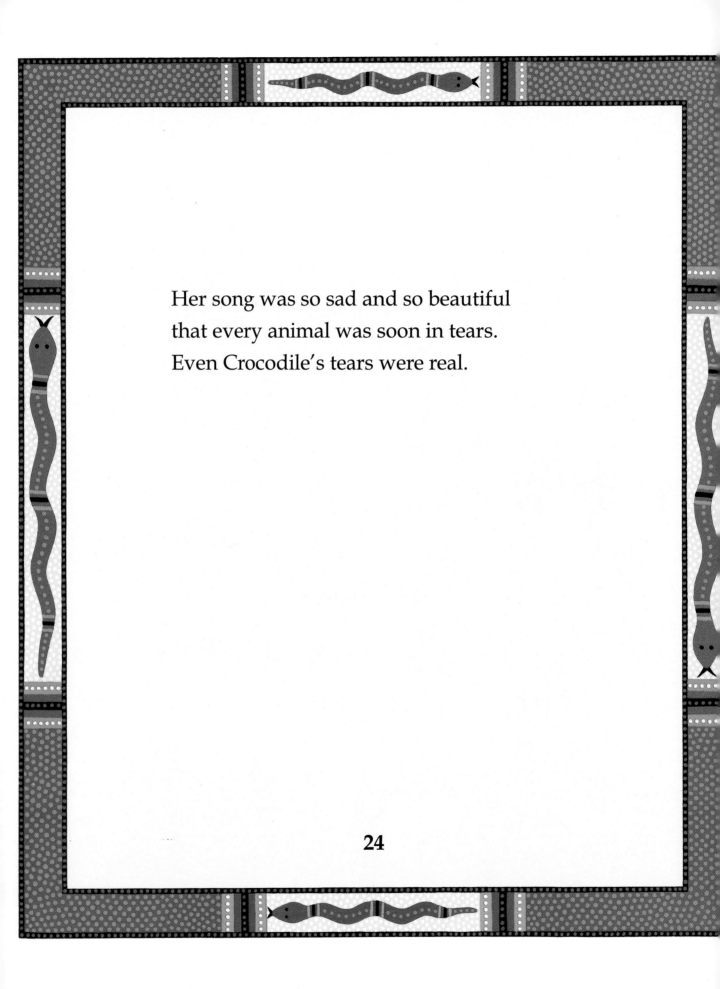

Her song was so sad and so beautiful
that every animal was soon in tears.
Even Crocodile's tears were real.

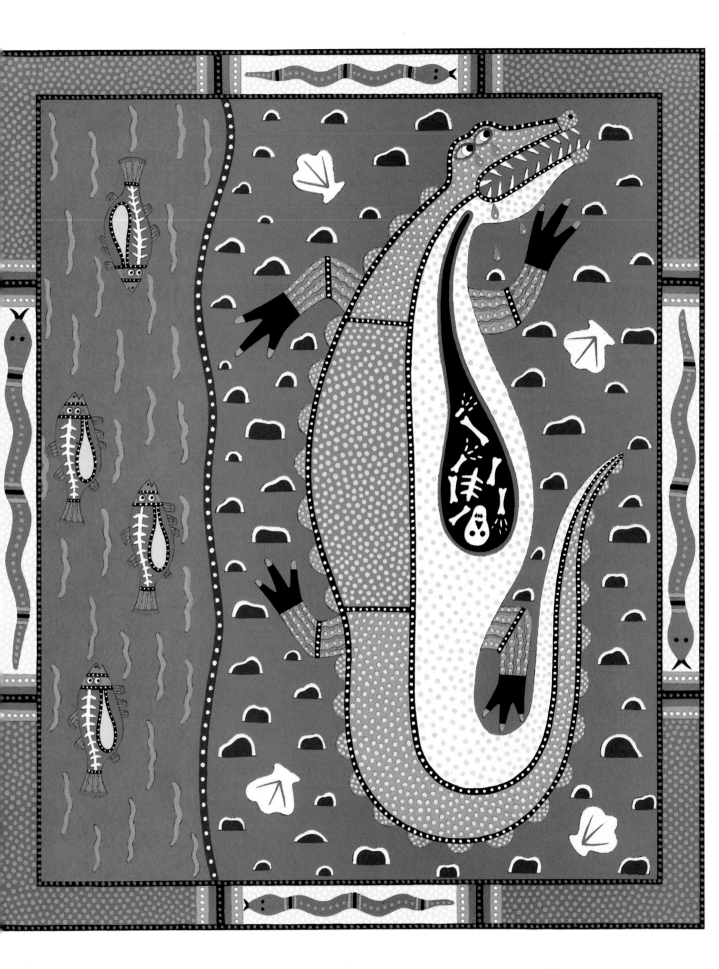

The other contestants agreed that Snake's song was so fine and his voice so perfect that he should win the contest. Red Spiny Lizard, Echidna, Honey Ant, Frilled Lizard, Kookaburra, Pelican, Frog, Wallaby, Lorikeet, Kangaroo, and the others did not even bother to compete.

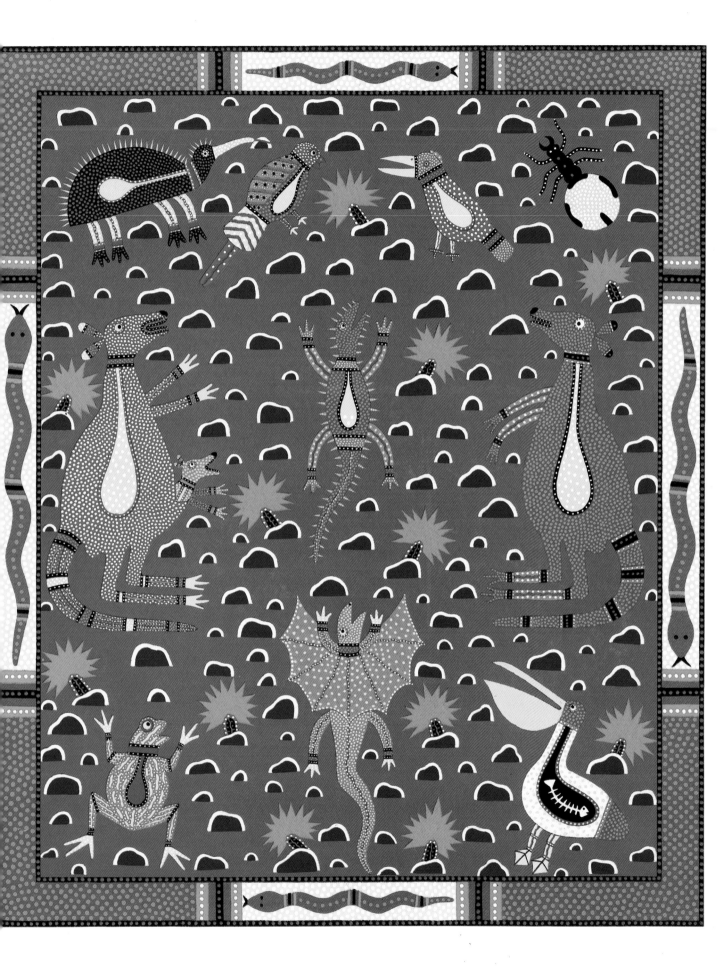

Old Man agreed and named Snake the
winner of the contest. "I will go now," he said,
"and make my musical instrument in Snake's
shape."

After Old Man had gone, the animals gathered around Snake. "Please, Snake, sing us an encore," they begged.

Snake smiled again. But this time, instead of singing, Lark began to scratch at Snake's throat with her little feet. Scratch, scratch. Scratch, scratch. Scratch, scratch.

Snake's cheeks bulged out as he tried not to cough. His eyes bulged, too. A faint sound like a hiss came from his mouth.

Lark continued to scratch with her little feet. Scratch, scratch. Scratch, scratch. Scratch, scratch.

Finally Snake could stand it no longer. With a loud hack, he coughed, and his mouth opened wide. Lark quickly flew to the safety of a tree branch and began to sing a glorious song of freedom.

All the creatures were so delighted with Lark's song that they were distracted for a moment. Snake quickly hid in another tree, pretending he was a branch.

When Lark's song was finished, the creatures noticed that Snake had disappeared. They were very angry. "He cheated us," they said. "He was horrible to Lark."

"We should never speak to him again," said Koala.

"Nor trust him," added Flying Squirrel.

When all the animals had gone, Snake came down from the tree. Just as he reached the ground, Old Man returned with his instrument.

"It looks like you, Snake," Old Man said, showing Snake the great horn that he had made. "The sound isn't as sweet as your singing, but I like it, and it will go well with your voice." Old Man blew into the strange instrument. A low, rich humming filled the air.

Snake said nothing and slithered off into the tall grass in shame.

No one ever did speak to Snake again.
After a while he forgot how to speak himself.
All he could make was a hissing sound, as if
something were going "scratch, scratch —
scratch, scratch" in his throat.

Today people call the island where these creatures lived Australia. They call the instrument the Old Man made a didgeridoo, and they refer to someone who cannot be trusted as a snake in the grass.

The didgeridoo is one of the oldest musical instruments known. It is made from a piece of tree trunk or limb with a soft center. The limb is thrown into a termite colony, and the termites eat out the center to make the limb hollow. Pitch and tone vary in accordance with the thickness of the wood. Didgeridoo players are required to constantly take in air through their nose as they blow continually with their mouth to play a tune.